# BATMAN

## THE MAKER OF MONSTERS

WRITTEN BY
ERIC FEIN

ILLUSTRATED BY
ERIK DOESCHER,
MIKE DECARLO, AND
LEE LOUGHRIDGE

BATMAN CREATED BY
BOB KANE

STONE ARCH BOOKS
a capstone imprint

Published by Stone Arch Books in 2011
A Capstone Imprint
151 Good Counsel Drive, P.O. Box 669
Mankato, Minnesota 56002
*www.capstonepub.com*

Cataloging-in-Publication Data is available on the Library of Congress website.

ISBN: 978-1-4342-1984-8 (library binding)
ISBN: 978-1-4342-2762-1 (paperback)

Summary: It's fall in Gotham. The air is getting colder, the leaves are changing
color, and the people are . . . turning into monsters! These evil creatures are
taking over the city, and the problem appears to be spreading. Luckily, Batman
and his crime-fighting partner, Robin, are investigating. The Dynamic Duo
traces the monster mess back to a local clinic, where the evil Hugo Strange
is turning his patients into troublesome terrors. The super heroes must work
together to put this monster medic out of business.

Art Director: Bob Lentz
Designer: Brann Garvey
Production Specialist: Michelle Biedscheid

Printed in the United States of America in Stevens Point, Wisconsin.
092010
005941R

# TABLE of CONTENTS

# CHAPTER 1

# MONSTER MASH

A full moon hung in the night sky over Gotham City. Its bright light gave the city a ghostly glow. In the theater district, the evening's shows had just ended, and theatergoers flooded the streets. All were in a hurry to get home. It was never good to be alone on the streets of Gotham at night.

"Wasn't that the greatest play ever?" said ten-year-old Johnny Dillon, walking away from the theater with his parents, Don and Mary. They were headed to the parking garage to pick up their car.

"It was frightful," Mary said, shivering. "I don't know what I was thinking when I agreed to let you pick the play. Did you have to choose the new Dracula musical? I'll have bad dreams for a month!"

"Come on, Mom, monsters are cool," Johnny said. "Don't be such a chicken —"

"Johnny!" snapped his father. "Don't tease your mother."

Before Johnny could apologize, a large shadow fell across the family. When they looked up, Mary screamed. Don's jaw nearly hit the street, and Johnny's eyes went wide with terror. Standing in front of them was a creature nine feet tall. Its skin was gray and thick and dry like leather. It wore hospital clothes, a dirty overcoat, and a wide-brimmed hat that covered the top half of his face.

"Daddy!" Johnny screamed.

"Easy," said Don, looking around for any signs of help. They were the only ones on the street. He grabbed Mary and Johnny by the arms. "Just step . . . back . . . slowly."

The monster cried out again and lunged toward the family. The beast raised its large hands as it drew closer.

"Run!" Don shouted.

The family quickly darted into an alleyway, but soon they reached a dead end. The monster was still close behind them.

"We're trapped!" Johnny said.

As the monster came toward them, Don stepped forward.

No one was going to hurt his family.

Suddenly, another shadow fell over them. A giant bat was soaring down from between the tall buildings. *Wait,* Don thought. *That's no bat, that's —*

"Batman!" Johnny shouted, pointing toward the sky.

Just then, the monster looked up. CRAAAAACK! Batman's boot heels struck its bony jaw. The creature crashed to the ground, and the Dark Knight landed and fired his grapnel gun. BANG! The grapnel's line wrapped around the monster, binding its arms to its side.

A red and black figure landed next to Batman. "Hey, save some fun for me," said Robin, the Dark Knight's super hero partner.

"Robin, get them out of the alley," Batman said.

"This way, folks," said Robin.

The family followed the Boy Wonder. As soon as they were on the street, the Dillons took off running.

Robin went back into the alley to find Batman facing the monster. It was on its feet again and struggling against the restraints. Suddenly, the beast roared and ripped the metal cord apart. *TWANNNGG!*

Batman aimed his grapnel gun at the monster again. The beast quickly leaped to its feet and knocked the gun out of Batman's hand. *CLANK!* It lunged at Batman, but the Dark Knight took a step back. As he did, he grabbed onto the front of the monster's coat.

The Dark Knight then pulled the monster forward. Batman positioned his feet against the monster's stomach. As Batman rolled backward, he kicked the creature up and over him. **CRASH!!** It landed in a nearby garbage dumpster.

"Nice move," Robin said.

**ROOAAARRR!!** The creature growled, quickly recovering and leaping from the dumpster.

"Can't this guy take a hint?" said Robin.

The Dynamic Duo ran out of the alleyway and onto the street, trying to figure out their next move.

"Any ideas how to stop Mr. Grumpy?" asked Robin.

Batman spotted a closed pizzeria with a large, neon light sign in the window.

"Yes," Batman said. "A bright idea. Why don't you check and see if our friend has any buddies nearby?"

"Right," Robin said, firing his grapnel gun into the air. The grapnel hook attached to a nearby building, and the super-strong wire quickly pulled him up to the roof.

Meanwhile, Batman led the monster toward the pizzeria, where it grabbed at him wildly. When he was in front of the restaurant, the Dark Knight stopped, and the monster approached slowly. It swung at Batman, but the Dark Knight easily dodged the blow. He jumped up and tapped the creature on the nose.

Angered, the creature charged at Batman again, but the Dark Knight jumped out of the way. He did a spinning back kick.

# SMAASSSHHHH!!

The kick sent the monster through the pizzeria's window and into the electrical sign. The shock from the sign knocked the beast out cold.

Batman stood over the downed creature, puzzled. "Who — or what — in the world are you?" he wondered aloud.

# CHAPTER 2

# A HORRIBLE CHANGE

The monster was still out cold on the street. Batman removed a small device from inside his Utility Belt. **FLASH!** He scanned the creature's fingerprints with it. The scanner was linked to the Batcomputer in the Batcave, which checked the prints against the ones it had on file. It was also connected to government computers all over the world.

A moment later, the scanner beeped. A match had been found. Batman was surprised by who the creature really was.

The scanner's view screen showed a man's picture and name. The information came from the U.S. Army. The man had served as a soldier twenty years ago. He was Jack "the Jolt" Jackson, a former all-star center fielder for the Gotham City Knights baseball team.

"Mr. Grumpy's working alone," Robin said, returning to the scene. "Did you find out who he is?"

Batman handed him the scanner.

"Whoa!" Robin exclaimed. "What happened to him?"

"That's what we are going to find out," Batman said. "Let's go."

The Dynamic Duo vanished into the night as the sound of police sirens filled the air.

The monster was taken to Gotham General Hospital. He was placed in a private room and strapped to a bed. Two officers stood guard outside of the door.

Police Commissioner James Gordon soon arrived. He stood in the hallway and spoke to Edward Ramos, the doctor in charge.

"What is it, Doctor?" asked Gordon.

"I don't have all the test results back yet, Commissioner," Dr. Ramos replied. "I would say that we are looking at a human male in his mid-forties. He's the victim of a very powerful drug. It caused his body to grow beyond its natural size."

"Is the patient awake?" said a voice from behind them.

The two men spun around. Batman was standing in the hallway, looking on.

"He's sleeping," Dr. Ramos said, surprised by Batman's arrival.

"Doctor, come quick!" shouted a nurse from the doorway to the monster's room.

Batman, Gordon, and Ramos ran into the room. They were joined by the police officers on guard duty. The monster, still tied down to his bed, was struggling to break free. SNAP! SMASH!

"He's trying to escape!" one of the police officers shouted.

"No," Batman said. "He's changing."

Batman was right. The monster *was* changing. It was becoming human again. The beast was growing smaller. Its skin lost the gray, leathery look.

Dr. Ramos went over to the man, placing his stethoscope to his chest.

"His heartbeat is fast but steady," Dr. Ramos said. "He seems to be okay for now."

Batman stepped over to the doctor. "I need to speak with him, Dr. Ramos," Batman said.

"No, he's too weak," the doctor said. "I can't allow it."

"This man could have important information about who did this to him," Batman insisted. "I need to question him."

"Doctor," Commissioner Gordon said, "please step outside with me."

The doctor and the others left the room, but Batman remained at the side of the bed. "Mr. Jackson," he said. "Can you tell me what happened to you?"

The man blinked. He was confused at first, but then his eyes quickly adjusted.

"Batman?" Jackson said. "What's going on? I feel like I was hit by a truck."

"You've had a wild night," Batman said. "You weren't yourself. What's the last thing you remember?"

"I checked in to the Houstan Health Clinic," Jackson said. "They treat sports injuries. I went to receive treatment for my shoulder pain. What happened tonight?"

"Somehow you were turned into a monster," Batman said. "You ran wild in the streets of Gotham."

"What?" Jackson said. "I would never hurt another person!"

"I know that, and don't worry — you didn't hurt anyone," Batman said.

"You have to clear my name, Batman," Jackson said.

"I run a charity organization that benefits Gotham's poor," he said. "I can't have this getting out to the public. If it does, my reputation will be destroyed. I won't be able to raise money for my charity."

"Rest easy, Mr. Jackson," Batman said. "I'll get to the bottom of this and clear your name. I promise."

# CHAPTER 3

# BAD MEDICINE

Later that night in the Batcave, the Dark Knight sat in his chair in front of the Batcomputer. Robin stood to his left. Alfred stood to his right. Batman had his mask pulled back, showing his true identity — Gotham City billionaire, Bruce Wayne.

"So what did you find?" asked Robin.

"The clinic Jackson went to, the Houstan Health Clinic, is something of a mystery," Batman said. "It seems to have sprung up out of the blue about six months ago. Doctor Greg Houstan runs it."

Batman continued. "He claims that his treatments can help damaged muscles heal faster than normal. I did a search for him but found very little information."

"You think it is a fake name, Master Bruce?" Alfred asked.

"Maybe," Batman said. He typed GREG HOUSTAN so that it appeared on the Batcomputer's screen. "Does anything about the name strike the two of you as *strange*?"

"If there is something, I don't see it," Alfred said.

"I don't either," Robin said.

"How about now?" Batman said. He mixed up the letters in the name. On the screen, the rearranged letters read: HUGO STRANGE.

"That mad scientist again?" said Robin.

"The one and only," Batman said.

"We're going to pay Strange a visit, aren't we?" Robin said.

"No," Batman replied. "This calls for a different approach. Alfred, gas up the Rolls Royce. Bruce Wayne is going to see if this Dr. Houstan can heal his tennis elbow."

"Very good, Master Bruce," Alfred said.

"What about me?" asked Robin.

"If I remember correctly," said Batman. "Tim Drake has a book report due on Monday, and you could use a little down time to finish it."

"You might need my help," Robin said.

Batman began to exit the room. "If I do, I'll call you," he said.

* * *

The clinic was ten miles outside of
Gotham City. The building looked like a
castle, and a heavy iron fence surrounded
the property. Alfred was behind the wheel
of the Rolls Royce, waiting for the electric
gate to open. When it did, he drove up to
the main building where a tall, muscular
man met them at the front door.

"I'll see you Sunday night, Alfred," Bruce
said. He grabbed his suitcase and got out of
the car.

"Welcome, Mr. Wayne. I am Bruno, Dr.
Houstan's assistant," the man said. "Follow
me. I'll take you to the doctor."

Dr. Houstan was a short man with thick
black hair. He sat behind a large oak desk
in an office lined with books.

"Thank you for seeing me on such short notice, Dr. Houstan," Bruce said, entering the office. "I'm supposed to play in a charity tennis match for the Gotham Orphanage. I guess I must have sprained my elbow during practice."

"Not to worry, Mr. Wayne. My treatment will have you back on the court in no time," replied the doctor. "But first, I need you to fill out these forms."

He slid a clipboard holding the forms over to Wayne. A pen sat on top of it. Bruce picked it up and began writing.

"We'll begin this afternoon," said the doctor. "You will receive a round of my own special vitamin shots. This will be followed by some basic body exercises. Finally, there will be sound and light treatments, which help my patients relax."

"Interesting," Bruce said.

Then suddenly, Bruce felt shaky. He tried to fill out the form but dropped the pen onto the floor. When he leaned over to pick it up, he lost his balance and crashed to the ground. **THUD!** His mind was racing. Dr. Houstan got up and walked around the desk. He stood over Bruce and snapped his fingers. Bruno walked in.

Bruce tried to get up but couldn't.

The doctor smiled. "No doubt you have many questions, Mr. Wayne," Dr. Houstan said. "Since you are my guest, I will be kind and answer them. A drug of my own making has frozen your muscles. The pen I gave you is coated with it. The drug entered your body through your skin."

"W-why?" Bruce asked, trembling.

Houstan stared at Wayne. "You rich people are all alike," he replied. "You think because you're rich and do good deeds that you're better than everyone else. But no one is beyond evil. I will show the world that you and your rich friends are just . . . monsters in disguise."

"You're out of your mind!" Bruce shouted, beginning to foam at the mouth.

"No, Mr. Wayne," Dr. Houstan said. He tore at his own face until chunks of it came off in his hands.

*A mask*, Bruce thought.

"I'm Dr. Hugo Strange," he said. "And soon, *you'll* be out of *your* mind."

# CHAPTER 4

# THE HERO WITHIN

A short time later, Bruce woke up chained to the wall in a dark lab. Hugo Strange walked over to him. The scientist held an injection gun.

"Ah, you're awake," Dr. Strange said. "Excellent. This won't hurt . . . much."

**CLICK!** He stuck a dart-like needle into Bruce's arm. "It will be a few minutes before the drug takes effect," said Dr. Strange. "Your body should handle it better than that ballplayer, Mr. Jackson. Something went wrong with him."

"He actually escaped before I could finish my experiments," Strange continued. "Still, I made my point, and he will now forever be viewed as a monster."

Bruce could feel the drug rushing through his body. His blood felt like it was boiling. His brain pounded in his head.

Dr. Strange smiled. "The change has begun," he said.

The doctor pressed a button on a nearby panel. **CLICK!** Bright lights circled the room, flashing in Bruce's eyes. Dr. Strange's voice boomed from every direction.

Bruce's body began to twist and tremble. He tried to force himself not to change, but it didn't work. His clothes began to rip and tear. The body he had spent years training to make perfect became oversized and ugly.

Bruce's thoughts grew fuzzy, and he wanted to say something but couldn't speak.

"That's right," Dr. Strange said. "Break free! Destroy the citizens of Gotham before they destroy you!"

The monster that was once Bruce Wayne roared and dived forward. The chains holding him snapped like strings of overcooked spaghetti. *SNAP! SNAP!*

Dr. Strange pointed to a wooden door. The Bruce Monster stared at it. Suddenly, the passageway opened, and Bruce ran into the tunnel. He was outside near the road to Gotham. The lights of the city's skyline glittered and gleamed.

*I am not a monster,* Bruce thought. *Why do I want to destroy things?*

Pain shot through his body. He drove his overgrown fists into the road, creating a large pothole. CRUNCH! Smashing things seemed to ease the pain.

The Bruce Monster ran toward Gotham, searching for more things to crush.

*   *   *

Meanwhile, Robin and Alfred were in the Batcave, listening to the police radio. They were watching the news for word of any new monster attacks.

"I don't like it, Alfred," said Robin. "Bruce didn't check in at the scheduled time. I think I should go to that clinic and have a look."

"Now, now," Alfred said. "Master Bruce probably has his reasons for waiting to call — Oh, my!"

On the TV, a newscast had a live feed from downtown Gotham. It showed a monster on the loose.

Robin jumped out of his chair.

"My word!" Alfred said.

"I'll handle this," said Robin. "You try to contact Bruce again."

Robin ran over to a row of Batcycles and jumped on one of them. He put on a helmet, pushed the starter button, and sped out of the Batcave.

ZWWWOOOOMMMM!

Within minutes, Robin had reached downtown Gotham City. He stopped the Batcycle in the middle of the street and listened. Soon, the young crime fighter heard what sounded like a stampede of cattle coming his way.

**AAAAAHHH!** Robin turned around and saw dozens of terrified citizens running for their lives. The monster chased them.

The Bruce Monster spotted Robin on his Batcycle. One part of him wanted to crush the young super hero. The other part of him knew this boy was a friend. He had to let Robin know what was going on. *But how?* wondered the Bruce Monster, unable to speak clearly. *How am I going to explain myself?*

At that moment, a car came to a stop in front of Bruce. As the driver hopped out and ran away, Bruce ripped off the car's hood. **CRUNCH!** He pulled out the oil tank and crushed it. The oil ran all over his fingers. Robin aimed his Batcycle right at the monster. However, he turned away as he realized what the creature was doing.

The monster was using an oil-dipped finger to draw something on the street. It was a picture of a bat. Its wings spread out just like Batman's chest symbol.

The monster looked at Robin. It pointed to the bat picture and then to itself.

"Batman? Is that you?" asked Robin.

The creature nodded.

"Come with me," Robin said. "We'll go to the Batcave so Alfred and I can help."

The Bruce Monster growled and shook its head. He pointed to where he came from.

"You want me to follow?" Robin asked, searching for more information.

The monster turned and ran. Robin followed on his Batcycle, hoping he wasn't riding into a trap.

# CHAPTER 5

# A STRANGE TWIST OF FATE

When he arrived in front of the clinic, Robin hid his Batcycle in some nearby bushes. As the Bruce Monster entered the main building, the Boy Wonder picked the lock to a side door and snuck inside. He heard the heavy footsteps of the Bruce Monster and followed them down the stairs to the clinic's lower level.

At the end of a long tunnel, Robin found himself at Strange's lab. He peeked in. Bruce had returned to normal, but he was weak. Bruno was chaining him to the wall.

"How did you like your first night as a monster, Mr. Wayne?" Dr. Strange said. "You should get used to it. I plan on giving you the drug every night for seven days. That's how long it takes to build up in your system. Once it does, you will be a monster forever. The only thing to keep you from changing will be this antidote."

Dr. Strange held up a small glass bottle filled with green liquid.

"However, I am willing to sell it to you," Strange said. "The price is only one hundred million dollars."

"Never!" Bruce said.

Dr. Strange smiled. "Fine, we'll see how tough you are in seven days," he said. He placed the bottle in a wall safe and then headed for the exit with Bruno.

Robin ducked into an empty room down the hall. When he was sure the two men were gone, he entered the lab. He unlocked Bruce's chains using a special key from his Utility Belt. **CLICK!**

"Quit hanging around, Bruce," teased Robin. "We have work to do."

"Hilarious," joked Bruce. "My suitcase is in the corner."

Robin got the case and tossed it to Bruce. He opened the false bottom within it and pulled out his Batman uniform.

Upstairs in Strange's office, an alarm was ringing. "Wayne is free!" Bruno shouted. "The chains are unlocked!"

"Fear not," said Dr. Strange. "I'll let some of our other millionaire monsters deal with him."

**BEEP!** Dr. Strange pushed a button on a control panel on his desk.

Downstairs, the doors to the cells swung open. Three shadowy figures stomped into the hallway. **THUD! THUD! THUD!**

Batman and Robin exited the lab. Suddenly, they found their way blocked by three gigantic monsters. The monster nearest Robin swung at him. **WHOOOOSH!** The Boy Wonder leaped out of the way.

"Put on your gas mask," Batman said.

They both took masks out of their Utility Belts. Then Batman fired his grapnel gun at the creatures, tangling all three of them together.

Robin then tossed some pills on the floor. **CLINK CLINK CLINK** They broke open, filling the tunnel with gas and smoke.

Soon, the creatures were unconscious. Batman and Robin dragged them back into one of the cells and locked the door.

"Watch out!" Batman said suddenly. He pushed Robin against the wall.

**ZING!** A needle filled with the monster drug flew past the Boy Wonder's head. Dr. Strange stood at the foot of the stairs holding another of his injection guns.

"You've messed up my plans," Dr. Strange said. He took aim again.

At the same time, Batman removed a Batarang from his Utility Belt and threw it.

**KKLLAAAANG!** The Batarang knocked the injection gun out of the doctor's hands — and into his own arm! Dr. Strange simply looked at it and blinked.

"Uh-oh," Robin said. "That's not good."

Strange was changing into a monster. However, instead of growing taller, the doctor grew shorter and wider. His back curved forward and his head hung at an angle. He took a couple of steps and then fell to the floor.

"Gurgle, gurgle," was all the blob-like Dr. Strange could manage to say.

"What happened to him?" Robin said.

Batman glanced at the now empty injection gun. "It looks like his body wasn't strong enough to handle such a high dose of the drug," he said.

*     *     *

The police arrived a short time later and found Bruno hiding in the woods. They took him, along with Dr. Strange, to Arkham Asylum.

Then Batman and Robin helped them load the other three monsters into a police van. They were taken to the hospital.

Afterward, Batman and Robin stood with Commissioner Gordon outside the clinic.

The Dark Knight handed Gordon the bottle that held the antidote. "Get this over to Wayne Enterprises," he said. "Wayne's scientists will copy it so you can cure Dr. Strange and his monsters."

Gordon pocketed the bottle. "Will do," he said, looking concerned. "But are you all right, Batman? You look a little worse for the wear tonight."

The Dark Knight flashed Gordon a tired smile. "It's been a *strange* evening, Commissioner," he said.

# Hugo Strange

**REAL NAME:** Doctor Hugo Strange

**OCCUPATION:** Psychologist

**BASE:** Gotham City

**HEIGHT:**
5 feet 10 inches

**WEIGHT:**
170 pounds

**EYES:**
Gray

**HAIR:**
None

The brilliant psychologist Dr. Hugo Strange invented a machine that could read and videotape a person's thoughts. Unfortunately, the greedy doctor used this ground-breaking technology to help himself instead of his patients. After recording the deepest, darkest secrets of his clients, Hugo Strange blackmailed them with the information. Then one day, he discovered the biggest secret of all — the true identity of Batman — making him one of the Dark Knight's most dangerous enemies.

# G.C.P.D. GOTHAM CITY POLICE DEPARTMENT

- Upon discovering Batman's secret identity, Hugo Strange attempted to auction off the information to the Joker, the Penguin, and Two-Face. However, the trio of super-villains didn't believe Bruce Wayne was Batman, so they tried to throw Dr. Strange out of a plane. A hero to all, Batman himself swooped in to save the mad doctor's life.

- Hugo Strange didn't give up. He later told Commissioner Gordon that Batman was Bruce Wayne, but Robin disguised himself as Batman, making it seem like Dr. Strange was wrong. Gordon then had him arrested.

- Dr. Strange has been known to use science as a weapon. He once infected Batman and Robin with a dangerous chemical. The drug caused the Dynamic Duo to hallucinate that they were being chased by zombies. Fortunately, Batgirl was able to give the two super heroes the antidote.

# CONFIDENTIAL

# BIOGRAPHIES

**Eric Fein** is a freelance writer and editor. He has written dozens of comic book stories featuring The Punisher, Spider-Man, Iron Man, and Conan. He has also written more than forty books and graphic novels for educational publishers. As an editor, Eric has worked on books featuring Spider-Man, Venom, and Batman, as well as several storybooks, coloring and activity books, and how-to-draw books.

**Erik Doescher** is a freelance illustrator and video game designer based in Dallas, Texas. He attended the School of Visual Arts in New York City. Erik illustrated for a number of comic studios throughout the 1990s, and then he moved to Texas to pursue videogame development and design. However, he has not completely given up on illustrating his favorite comic book characters.

**Mike DeCarlo** is a longtime contributor of comic art whose range extends from Batman and Iron Man to Bugs Bunny and Scooby-Doo. He resides in Connecticut with his wife and four children.

**Lee Loughridge** has been working in comics for more than fifteen years. He currently lives in sunny California in a tent on the beach.

# GLOSSARY

**antidote** (AN-ti-dote)—something that stops a poison from working

**apologize** (uh-POL-uh-jize)—to say that you are sorry about something

**charity** (CHA-ruh-tee)—a group that gives money to people in need

**identity** (eye-DEN-ti-tee)—your identity is who you are as a person

**reputation** (rep-you-TAY-shuhn)—your worth or character, as judged by other people

**restraint** (ri-STRAYNT)—a device that restricts movement, such as a rope or handcuffs

**stampede** (stam-PEED)—a wild rush of frightened animals moving in one direction

**stethoscope** (STETH-uh-skope)—a medical instrument used by doctors to listen to the sound from a patient's heart and lungs

**Utility Belt** (yoo-TIL-uh-tee BELT)—Batman's belt, which holds all of his weaponry and gadgets

# DISCUSSION QUESTIONS

1. Robin and Batman teamed up to take down Dr. Strange. Which super hero do you think played a bigger role in defeating the mad scientist?

2. What does it take to be a hero? What kinds of heroic things does Batman do in this book?

3. This book has ten illustrations. Which one is your favorite? Why?

# WRITING PROMPTS

1. When Bruce Wayne turned into a monster, he had to struggle to keep control of himself. Have you ever had trouble controlling yourself? What happened? Write about your difficult experience.

2. Batman can always count on his butler, Alfred, to help him out when he is in trouble. Who do you count on for help?

3. Imagine that you've been turned into a monster! What kind of creature would you become? What kinds of powers would you have? Draw a picture of your new form.

WAIT!!
DON'T CLOSE THE BOOK!
THERE'S MORE!
FIND MORE:
GAMES & PUZZLES
HEROES & VILLAINS
AUTHORS & ILLUSTRATORS
AT...
WWW.CAPSTONEKIDS.COM
STILL WANT MORE?
FIND COOL WEBSITES AND MORE BOOKS LIKE THIS ONE AT WWW.FACTHOUND.COM. JUST TYPE IN THE BOOK ID: 9781434219848 AND YOU'RE READY TO GO!

# MORE NEW BATMAN ADVENTURES!

**KILLER CROC HUNTER**

**SCARECROW, DOCTOR OF FEAR**

**MAD HATTER'S MOVIE MADNESS**

**CATWOMAN'S HALLOWEEN HEIST**

**ROBIN'S FIRST FLIGHT**